Tillie and the Wall

Tillie
and
the Wall

Leo Lionni

Dragonfly Books
New York

The wall had been there ever since the mice could remember. They never paid attention to it. They never asked themselves what was on the other side, nor, for that matter, if there was another side at all. They went about their business as if the wall didn't exist.

The mice loved to talk. They chatted endlessly about this and that, but no one ever mentioned the wall. Only Tillie, the youngest, would stare at it, wondering about the other side.

At night, while the others were asleep, she would lie in her bed of straw, wide awake, imagining beyond the wall a beautiful, fantastic world inhabited by strange animals and plants.

"We *must* see the other side," she told her friends. "Let us try to climb." They tried, but as they climbed, the wall seemed higher and higher.

With a long, rusty nail they tried to make a hole to peep through. "It is only a question of patience!" said Tillie. But after working an entire morning they gave up, exhausted, without having made even a dent in the hard stone.

"The wall must end *somewhere*," Tillie said. They walked and walked for many hours. The wall apparently had no end.

But one day, not far from the wall, Tillie saw a worm digging itself into the black earth. How could she not have thought of that before? Why hadn't anyone thought of that before?

Full of excitement, Tillie began to dig. She
dug and she dug . . .

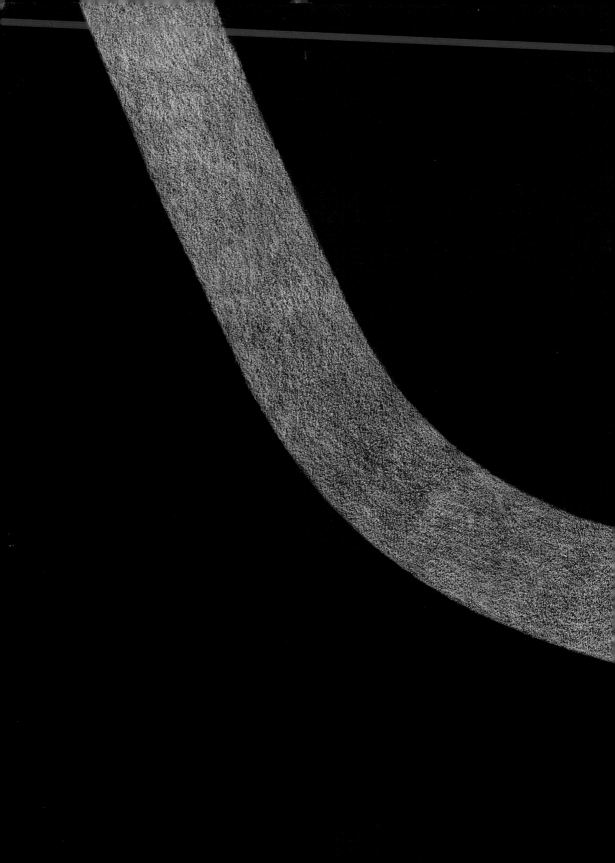

until suddenly, almost blinded by the bright sunlight, she was on the other side of the wall! She couldn't believe her eyes: before her were mice, regular mice.

The mice gave Tillie a great welcome party.
They took her to their celebration pebble
(had she seen that before somewhere?).
They made speeches in her honor and waved
flags.

They then decided to go through Tillie's tunnel to see for themselves what the other side was like. One by one they followed Tillie.

And when the mice on Tillie's side of the wall saw what Tillie had discovered, there was another party. The mice threw confetti. Everyone shouted "TIL-LIE, TIL-LIE, TIL-LIE!" and they carried Tillie high in the air in triumph.

Since that day the mice go freely from one side of the wall to the other, and they always remember that it was Tillie who first showed them the way.

About the Author

Leo Lionni, an internationally known designer, illustrator, and graphic artist, was born in Holland and studied in Italy until he came to the United States in 1939. He was the recipient of the 1984 American Institute of Graphic Arts Gold Medal and was honored posthumously in 2007 with the Society of Illustrators Lifetime Achievement Award. His picture books are distinguished by their enduring moral themes, graphic simplicity, and brilliant use of collage, and include four Caldecott Honor Books: *Inch by Inch*, *Frederick*, *Swimmy*, and *Alexander and the Wind-Up Mouse*. Hailed as "a master of the simple fable" by the *Chicago Tribune*, he died in 1999 at the age of 89.

Copyright © 1989 by Leo Lionni

All rights reserved. Published in the United States by Dragonfly Books, an imprint of Random House Children's Books, a division of Random House, Inc., New York. Originally published in hardcover in the United States by Alfred A. Knopf, an imprint of Random House Children's Books, a division of Random House, Inc., New York, in 1989.

Dragonfly Books with the colophon is a registered trademark of Random House, Inc.

Visit us on the Web! www.randomhouse.com/kids

Educators and librarians, for a variety of teaching tools, visit us at www.randomhouse.com/teachers

The Library of Congress has cataloged the hardcover edition of this work as follows:
Lionni, Leo.
Tillie and the wall.
Summary: Unlike the other mice, who are incurious about the wall that has always been part of their world, Tillie is determined to find out what lies on the other side of the wall.
ISBN 978-0-394-82155-9 (trade) — ISBN 978-0-394-92155-6 (lib. bdg.)
[1. Mice—Fiction.] I. Title. PZ7.L6634Tj 1989 [E] 88009316

ISBN 978-0-679-81357-6 (pbk.)

MANUFACTURED IN CHINA
15 14 13 12